This Walker book belongs to

_____

_____

_____

For splish-splash-sploshers
everywhere! ~ E.P.

For Raya ~ C.A.

**WALKER BOOKS**
AND SUBSIDIARIES
LONDON · BOSTON · SYDNEY · AUCKLAND

First published 2022 by Walker Books Ltd, 87 Vauxhall Walk, London SE11 5HJ

This edition published 2022 for Scottish Book Trust · Scottish charity SC027699

10 9 8 7 6 5 4 3 2 1

Text © 2022 Emma Perry · Illustrations © 2022 Claire Alexander

The right of Emma Perry and Claire Alexander to be identified as author and illustrator respectively
of this work has been asserted in accordance with the Copyright, Designs and Patents Act 1988

This book has been typeset in Burbank Regular · Printed in China

British Library Cataloguing in Publication Data: a catalogue record for this book is available from the British Library

ISBN 978-1-5295-1360-8

www.walker.co.uk

MIX
Paper from
responsible sources
FSC® C020056

# PUDDLING!

Emma Perry Illustrated by Claire Alexander

Clouds gather,
Skies darken,
Rain drops,
Puddles appear.

"Let's go!"

Drops race
Down the glass,
Nose pressed,
Which wins?
"Let's go..."

Wellies on,
Coat zipped,
Hood up.

Open door,

Open gate,

Hug, hug, hug!

"Let's ALL go ...

PUDDLING!"

Drenched dog
Stops still,
Shakes head,
Shakes body.

# Watch out! Water flying ...
# EVERYWHERE!

"Let's keep puddling!"

Stimp,

Stamp,

Stomp!

Umbrellas fly,
Coats flap,
Hats cover
Busy people
Missing fun.

# Look out, rushing past ...

big bike, big puddle.

SPLAAASH!

"Let's keep puddling!"

Splish,

Splash,

Splosh!

Muddy puddles, teeny puddles.

UH-OH!

HUMONGOUS puddle,
DEEP puddle,
Wellies ...

# FULL!

Squish!

Squash!

Squelch!

Socks soggy,
Toes cold.

"Let's go back!"

Open gate, open door.

**Emma Perry** is a children's book author, a primary school teacher, the founder of the children's book review site My Book Corner, and she also runs International Book Giving Day. She has written *I Don't Like Books. Never. Ever. The End.*, illustrated by Sharon Davey, and *This Book Has Alpacas and Bears*, illustrated by Rikin Parekh. She lives with her husband, her two children and two cats, and enjoys growing wonky vegetables in an allotment. Find her online at www.emmaperryauthor.com, on Instagram as @emmaperry and on Twitter as @_EmmaPerry.

**Claire Alexander** is an author and illustrator with a number of picture books to her name, including her author-illustrated books *The Think-Ups!* and *A Little Bit Different*, and *Humperdink* and *The Snowbear*, both written by Sean Taylor. In 2007, Claire began teaching courses and masterclasses on how to create a picture book, which she continues to run at the House of Illustration. Find Claire online at www.clairealexander.co.uk, on Instagram as @claire_alexander_picture_books and on Twitter as @PicBookCourse.